SCOOBY-DOO! ™

AND THE FRANKENSTEIN MONSTER

Look for the **Scooby-Doo Mysteries**.
Set 2:

SCOOBY-DOO! AND THE FRANKENSTEIN MONSTER

Written by
James Gelsey

For Helen

visit us at www.abdopublishing.com

Reinforced library bound edition published in 2013 by Spotlight, a division of the ABDO Group, PO Box 398166, Minneapolis, MN 55439. Spotlight produces high-quality reinforced library bound editions for schools and libraries. Published by agreement with Warner Bros.-A Time Warner Company.

Printed in the United States of America, North Mankato, Minnesota.
102012
012013
♻This book contains at least 10% recycled materials.

Cover and interior illustrations by Duendes Del Sur.

Library of Congress Cataloging-in-Publication Data
This book was previously cataloged with the following information:

Gelsey, James.
Scooby-doo! and the Frankenstein monster / written by James Gelsey.
p. cm. -- (Scooby-Doo Mysteries)
Scooby and the gang try to keep a monster in a wax museum from stealing a rare necklace.
[1. Dogs--Fiction. 2. Detective and mystery stories.]

2002567909

ISBN 978-1-61479-043-3 (reinforced library bound edition)

All Spotlight books are reinforced library bindings
and manufactured in the United States of America.

Chapter 1

"Hey, Fred," Shaggy called from the back of the Mystery Machine. "Do we have time for a quick lunch?"

"Shaggy, we just had lunch," Daphne said.

"That explains why Scoob and I are still hungry," Shaggy said.

"What are you talking about?" Velma asked. "Each of you ate two helpings of everything."

"Yeah, but we usually eat three of every-thing," Shaggy replied.

"Oh, brother," Daphne moaned.

5

Fred steered the Mystery Machine into an empty parking lot. He turned off the engine.

"Here we are, gang," said Fred. "Madame Gaspacho's Wax Museum."

"Like, it looks like we're the first ones here," Shaggy said.

"Actually, we're the only ones here," Velma corrected.

"The only ones?" Shaggy asked.

"Rikes!" Scooby barked. He slid under the seat in the van.

"What's gotten into you two?" Daphne asked.

"Like, these places give me the creeps," Shaggy explained.

"Reah, the reeps," Scooby echoed.

"It's all those wax people," Shaggy continued. "They look like they're gonna come to life any minute."

"That's what makes them so amazing," Daphne said.

"Madame Gaspacho's Wax Museum is world famous," Velma added. "We're lucky that Daphne's uncle was able to get us in while it's closed."

"And why exactly do we want to go while it's closed?" Shaggy asked.

Fred, Velma, and Daphne looked at one another and rolled their eyes.

"Because Her Royal Highness Countess Cassandra is coming to the museum today," Daphne explained. "We're going to watch how her wax statue is made."

"It looks like we're not the only ones watching," Shaggy said. "Look."

The gang watched a tall figure walk around the corner. He wore a long dark overcoat with its collar hiding his face. He carried a small black bag over his shoulder. He looked around before he knocked on the museum's door. A moment later, the door opened and he walked inside.

"Talk about creepy," Daphne said. "Whoever that was looked awfully strange."

"And very mysterious," Velma added.

"Well, gang, we don't have much time," Fred said. "What do you say we go inside?"

"Great idea, Fred," Velma said.

Fred, Daphne, and Velma stepped out of the van.

"Shaggy? Scooby?" Daphne called. "Aren't you two coming?"

"Ro ranks, Raphne," Scooby barked.

"Scooby-Doo and I will stay here where we don't have to worry about running into creepy-looking men wearing long trench coats," Shaggy added.

"Okay, but there might be a snack bar inside," Daphne said. "See you later." Fred, Daphne, and Velma walked toward the museum entrance.

"Rack rar?" Scooby barked.

"I'm with you, pal," Shaggy said. "Let's go!"

Chapter 2

The gang stood outside the wax museum's door. Fred tried to open it, but it was locked.

"I guess we'd better knock," he said. He knocked on the door just like the mysterious stranger had.

A few moments later, they heard a click and the door opened. A woman dressed in a bright red gown stood before them.

"May I help you?" she asked.

"Good afternoon, Madame Gaspacho," Daphne said. "I'm Daphne Blake. I believe my uncle called you about my friends and me coming by to see the museum today."

"Oh, goodness, yes, children," the woman said, smiling. "Do come in. Quickly." Before she closed the door, the woman peered out to see if anyone else was there. Then she quickly pulled the door closed and locked it. She put the key on a chain around her neck.

"I'm Madame Gaspacho," the woman said. "Welcome to my wax museum."

"Thank you," Daphne said. "These are my friends: Fred, Velma, Shaggy, and Scooby-Doo."

"Pleased to meet you," Madame Gaspa-

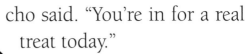

cho said. "You're in for a real treat today."

"Treats?" Shaggy asked. "As in snacks?"

"Better than that," she replied.

Madame Gaspacho led the gang through the lobby area and down a long hallway. The sides of the hallway were lined with wax figures from different periods of history.

"Look, there's George Washington," Velma pointed out.

"And there's Thomas Edison," Fred said.

"And Eleanor Roosevelt," Daphne added. "They look so lifelike."

"Thank you, my dear," Madame Gaspacho replied. "I pride myself on the high-quality wax statues in my museum. Some people think they've even seen them come to life."

"C-c-c-come to life?" Shaggy asked.

12

"Certainly," said Madame Gaspacho. As she walked, she pointed to the different wax figures. "Guests have told me they've seen Albert Einstein blink. And Betsy Ross sew. And Henry the Eighth eat."

Shaggy and Scooby stopped in their tracks in front of Henry the Eighth. He was holding a giant turkey drumstick in one hand.

"Hey, Scoob, what do you think wax statues eat?" Shaggy asked.

"Randles!" Scooby barked.

Shaggy and Scooby laughed. "Candles.

That's funny, Scoob," Shaggy said. "Hey, where'd everyone else go?" They looked around and noticed they were alone.

"I was afraid something like this would happen," Shaggy said. "Let's keep going. You watch the statues on that side of the hall. I'll watch the ones on this side."

"Rokay!" Scooby barked.

Shaggy and Scooby slowly continued along the hallway. They kept their eyes on the wax statues as they walked. Then — BUMP! Shaggy and Scooby walked into a wax statue. It stood right in the middle of the hallway.

The figure was dressed in a black suit with a black shirt. It had a mean-looking face with dark eyes and thin, tight lips. A small black bag hung over its left shoulder.

"Zoinks!" Shaggy exclaimed. "What a creepy-looking guy!"

"Reah, reepy," Scooby agreed.

They continued walking down the hallway.

"Hey, Scoob," Shaggy said. "Get your hot

breath off my neck, will you?"

"Ruh?" Scooby said. Shaggy looked over and saw Scooby walking next to him.

"Scoob, if you're not behind me, who's breathing on me?" Shaggy asked.

He and Scooby turned and saw the creepy wax figure standing right behind them.

"Rikes!" Scooby barked.

"Zoinks!" Shaggy shouted. "Like, let's get

out of here! Like, fast as we can!"

Shaggy and Scooby ran the rest of the way down the hall.

"Heeeeeeeelllllppppp!"

Chapter 3

Madame Gaspacho was showing Fred, Daphne, and Velma the "Royalty Room."

"Help! He's after us!" Shaggy shouted. He and Scooby ran into the room and dived behind an enormous throne.

"What's going on?" Fred asked. "Shaggy? Scooby?"

"One of the wax thingies came to life and chased me and Scooby," Shaggy said from behind the throne. "He's probably behind you right now!"

Everyone turned and saw a tall man in

black stroll into the room. He had a slight smile on his face.

"Everything all right, Mr. Tock?" Madame Gaspacho asked.

"Yes," the man replied. "I think I may have frightened two of your guests."

Madame Gaspacho looked at Fred, Daphne, and Velma. "You can tell your friends to come out now," she said.

"Shaggy, Scooby, come out from behind that throne," Velma said. "Here's your wax thingie."

Shaggy and Scooby peeked over the top of the throne.

"That's him! He's alive!" Shaggy exclaimed.

"Of course I'm alive," Mr. Tock said. "I wouldn't be of much use to the countess if I weren't."

"Countess Cassandra?" Daphne asked.

"That would be me," came a voice from behind one of the wax figures.

"Zoinks! There's another one!" Shaggy exclaimed. He and Scooby jumped behind Fred, Daphne, and Velma.

A woman walked out from behind the display. She wore a very elegant dress. And an enormous diamond necklace sparkled around her neck. A man in a long white lab coat followed her. He carried a small black bag over his shoulder.

"Allow me to present Her Royal Highness Countess Cassandra," Madame Gaspacho said.

The gang couldn't believe their eyes.

"It is an honor to meet you," Daphne said. She and Velma curtsied.

"Yes, a true honor," Fred added. He bowed his head and gestured to Shaggy and Scooby to do the same.

19

"Please, please, no formalities," the countess said. "Madame Gaspacho told me a group of young people would be here today. It's a privilege to meet you."

"Thank you, Countess," Daphne replied. "It's a privilege for us as well."

"And this is Mr. Tock," the countess said. "My personal bodyguard."

The man in the white lab coat then cleared his throat.

"I'm sorry, Brant," Madame Gaspacho said. "Excuse me, everyone. This is Brant Embers, my artist in residence."

"Like, what does that mean?" Shaggy asked.

"She means that he's the man who creates all of the wax statues," Velma explained.

20

"And he's working on a statue of the countess even as we speak," Madame Gaspacho added.

"Excuse me," Mr. Tock interrupted. "It is getting late, Countess. We have several more appointments today."

"Of course, Mr. Tock, but I do wish to see a little more of the wax museum," the countess said. "Madame Gaspacho, can you and Mr. Embers give me a quick tour?"

"It would be my pleasure," Madame Gaspacho replied. "But Mr. Embers needs to finish perfecting your wax figure. I'm sure you understand."

"Certainly," the countess said. She looked at the gang. "Would you care to join me?" she asked.

"I must register my strong disagreement with this change in your schedule, Countess," Mr. Tock said. "You are making it very hard for me to do my job."

"Then perhaps you should find another job, Tock," the countess replied.

"Yes, well, then . . . I will phone the driver and tell him to wait," Mr. Tock said. He took a cell phone from his black bag and walked away.

"Shall we, Countess?" Madame Gaspacho asked. She and the countess walked into the next room.

"Let's go, gang," Fred said. "We don't want to miss this."

"No one should have to miss this," Brant said unhappily.

"Is everything all right, Mr. Embers?" Daphne asked.

"It's just that Madame Gaspacho takes credit for all of my creations," Brant replied. "And now she won't even let me walk around the museum to show off my artwork."

"You're right, that isn't very nice," Daphne said.

"I wonder if she's afraid your being there will take attention away from her?" Velma said.

"I'll give her something to be afraid of, just you wait!" Brant turned and disappeared through a door at the back of the exhibit.

"I sure don't like the sound of that," Fred said.

"Let's go catch up with the countess before she leaves," Daphne said. "This is a once-in-a-lifetime opportunity."

Chapter 4

The gang walked into the next room. It contained an exhibit of famous sports figures. The countess was looking at some of the baseball players.

"Which one of these is Babe Ruth?" the countess asked. "My grandfather used to tell me wonderful stories about him."

"Right over there, Countess," Madame Gaspacho said. She pointed to a stocky wax figure in a baseball uniform.

"Smile, everyone!" came a voice from Babe Ruth.

"Zoinks! Another talking dummy!"

Shaggy exclaimed.

A man holding a camera jumped out from behind Babe Ruth. A black bag hung over his right shoulder.

"I'm no dummy," the man said. "Just a photographer."

He raised his camera to take a picture. He pressed the shutter button but nothing happened.

"Rats!" the man said. "What's wrong with this thing?" Just as he turned the camera around to look at it, the flash went off.

"Hank Harberg!" Madame Gaspacho yelled. "I warned you about sneaking up on us like that!"

"You know I do my best work with the el-
ement of surprise," Hank said.

"Who is this man?" the countess asked.

"This is the reporter I told you about,
Countess," Madame Gaspacho replied. "He's
here to do a story on the museum for his
newspaper."

Hank gave a slight bow as he introduced
himself.

"I'm Hank Harberg, Countess," Hank

said. "Sorry if I startled you. Just doing my job. Now, how about a picture?"

Hank put his camera bag down and raised the camera to his eye.

"I'm very flattered, Mr. Harberg," the countess said, "but no thank you." She turned and looked at the "Heroes of the Olympics" display.

"I gotta have a picture," Hank said. "How about one of you and the kids? Or one of that nifty necklace you're wearing? That'll sell some papers."

"You heard the countess," Madame Gaspacho said. "You're here to do a story on the wax museum. Feel free to walk around by yourself, but please leave the countess alone." Madame Gaspacho led the countess to another exhibit.

"Can you believe her?" Hank said. "I'll bet the countess gets her picture taken all the time."

"Maybe that's why she wants to be left alone," Daphne suggested.

"One more wouldn't kill her," Hank said, "and it would help me keep my job. The only reason I agreed to come was to get a story about the countess. And if she won't cooperate, I'll just have to find a story without her help!"

As Hank walked away, he tripped over his camera bag. He stood up, picked up the bag, and left the gang all by themselves.

"He sure didn't sound very happy," Daphne said.

"Like, maybe he's in a bad mood 'cause he didn't eat lunch yet," Shaggy said. "Speaking of lunch, Scoob, let's go find that snack bar." He and Scooby walked out of the exhibit room.

A second later, a bloodcurdling scream filled the museum. Shaggy and Scooby ran back into the room.

"We didn't do it! We didn't do it!" Shaggy called.

"It sounded like it came from down there," Fred said. "Come on, gang!"

Chapter 5

The gang ran through the museum and into the "Movie Monsters" exhibit. The countess was lying on the floor. Her head was on Madame Gaspacho's lap.

"What happened, Madame Gaspacho?" Velma asked.

"I'm not sure, really," Madame Gaspacho said. "All I know is that I was over there combing the Wolfman's hair. The countess was over here somewhere and then I heard her scream. I turned and saw her fall to the floor."

"Quick, call an ambulance," Fred said.

"Wait just a moment," a man said. Everyone turned and saw Mr. Tock standing in the doorway. He ran over to the countess and nudged Madame Gaspacho out of the way. He reached into his pocket and removed a small vial of smelling salts. He broke open the vial and waved it under the countess's nose.

"Countess? Countess?" he said.

The countess suddenly coughed and opened her eyes.

"Get some water," ordered Mr. Tock.

"No, I'm all right, really," the countess said. Mr. Tock helped her stand up.

Brant Embers ran through a door at the back of the exhibit.

"Is everything all right?" he asked. "Who screamed?"

"What happened, Countess?" Madame Gaspacho asked.

"You're not going to believe this," the countess said. "I was looking at the Frankenstein's monster when it started moving. I

wasn't alarmed, because I know that many of the figures move a little bit. But then it walked right over to me. It reached out its hand and grabbed my necklace. As soon as I screamed, it ripped the necklace from around my neck. That's when I must have fainted."

"You m-m-m-mean the F-F-F-Frankenstein's monster is alive?" Shaggy asked.

"I think so," the countess replied.

"We're leaving this very minute," Mr. Tock said.

"Great, can Scoob and I have a ride?" Shaggy asked.

"We can't go anyplace," the countess replied.

"Why not?" asked Mr. Tock.

"Yeah, why not?" echoed Shaggy.

"Because Frankenstein's monster has my necklace," the countess said.

"It's just an imitation," Mr. Tock said.

"Why are you so worried?"

"Because it's not an imitation," the countess replied. "I wanted Mr. Embers to capture the true brilliance of the necklace in all of its splendor. That's why I decided to wear the real necklace today instead. So we can't leave until we find Frankenstein's monster — and my necklace."

"Just my luck," Hank exclaimed as he ran into the room. He fiddled with his camera as he spoke. "Frankenstein's monster steals the countess's necklace and I miss the whole thing. How about a couple of pictures showing the countess's despair?"

"No pictures," Mr. Tock said firmly.

"Madame Gaspacho," Fred asked, "can

anyone get in or out of the museum?"

"Not without this," Madame Gaspacho replied. She showed Fred the key around her neck.

"That means that Frankenstein's monster must still be in the museum someplace," Fred said. "Gather 'round, gang." The gang huddled up.

"Countess, perhaps you should rest in my office," Madame Gaspacho suggested.

"An excellent idea," Mr. Tock added. "I will search for the necklace."

"That won't be necessary, Mr. Tock," Velma said. "The Mystery, Inc., gang is on the case!"

Chapter 6

"I'm not going to let a bunch of kids search for one of the most valuable jewels in the world," Mr. Tock exclaimed. "I will take care of everything, Countess. Do not worry." Mr. Tock stormed out of the room.

"Countess, let's go to my office now," Madame Gaspacho said. "I'll brew up a nice cup of tea."

"Thank you, Madame Gaspacho," the countess said.

"Hank, be a dear and help," Madame Gaspacho said.

"Only if I can get an exclusive story," Hank

36

said. He put his camera over his shoulder and escorted the countess out of the room.

"Do you kids need a hand?" Brant asked.

Just as Fred was about to answer, Madame Gaspacho poked her head through the doorway.

"Don't you have some work to do on the countess's wax statue, Brant?" she asked. "We need to have that statue ready for tomorrow. Just think of the publicity!"

Brant mumbled under his breath as he turned and walked away.

"Okay, gang, there's no time to waste," Fred said. "If we're going to solve this mystery soon, we'd better split up."

"Good idea, Fred," Velma said. "Shaggy, Scooby, and I will start in here."

"And Daphne and I will see what that door leads to," Fred said. He pointed to the door at the back of the exhibit. "It seems that there's a door just like it at the back of every exhibit room."

Fred and Daphne opened the door and walked inside.

"Shaggy, you and Scooby look over there," Velma said, pointing. "I'll look over here. And remember: The faster we solve this mystery, the sooner you two can go eat."

"Say no more, Velma," Shaggy said. He and Scooby quickly walked over to the other section.

"Like, look at all these monsters," Shaggy said. "There's Dracula." Shaggy ran behind the wax figure of Dracula.

"I vant to eat your Scooby Snacks," Shaggy said in Dracula's voice. "Ah-ah-ah."

Scooby giggled. Then he ran behind the Wolfman.

"Raaaaaaa-wooooooo," Scooby howled from behind the wax figure.

"That sounds great, Scooby," Shaggy said. "How about this?"

Shaggy ran behind the Mummy.

"I want my deaddy," Shaggy moaned. "Get it? Mummy and Deaddy?"

Shaggy and Scooby laughed out loud. They laughed so hard they couldn't see where they were going. Scooby suddenly tripped on something.

"Hey, Scoob, you okay?" Shaggy asked.

"Ri rink ro," Scooby replied.

"Looks like you tripped on a pair of legs, that's all," Shaggy said. Shaggy and Scooby looked at each other. "A pair of legs?"

"Ru-huh." Scooby nodded.

"Velma!" Shaggy called. "We found something! Or somebody! Or part of somebody!"

Velma ran over.

"What is it?" she asked. "What did you find?"

Shaggy pointed to the legs. Velma knelt down for a closer look.

"Hmmm, you found a body, all right," Velma confirmed. "Only it's not alive."

"I was afraid of that," Shaggy moaned.

"In fact, it never was alive," Velma said. "Look." She held up the Frankenstein's monster's head.

"Zoinks!" Shaggy exclaimed. "It's — it's Frankenstein's monster!"

"Rikes!" Scooby jumped into Shaggy's arms.

"It's only the wax head of Frankenstein's monster," Velma explained. "It looks like our jewel-stealing monster hid the wax Frankenstein's monster over here. He must have taken the clothes off the wax dummy."

Velma then looked more closely at the floor.

"What's this?" she said. Velma bent over and picked something up.

"Velma, like, are you sure this is the right time to be putting on lipstick?" Shaggy asked.

"This isn't my lipstick," Velma said. "It's green, the same color as this Frankenstein's monster's face. Very interesting. Now let's see if the monster left any more clues. Follow me."

Velma got up and walked into the next exhibit room.

"Hey, Scooby-Doo," Shaggy called. "Think fast!" Shaggy tossed the wax monster head into the air. Before Scooby could catch it, a hand reached out and grabbed the wax head.

Shaggy and Scooby looked up. It was the real Frankenstein's monster!

"Arrrrrrrrrrrrgggggghhhhhhhh!" the monster growled at them.

"Let's get out of here, Scoob!" Shaggy yelled.

Chapter 7

Shaggy and Scooby ran into the next room.

"Make way!" Shaggy yelled.

He and Scooby ran right into the "Inventors" exhibit.

"Quick, in here, Scooby," Shaggy said. He and Scooby jumped into the Model T Ford on display. They hid under a blanket in the car.

"Do you think he's gone?" Shaggy whispered a moment later.

"Robably," Scooby whispered back.

"Why are you whispering?" a voice asked.

"Ahhhhhhhh!" Shaggy and Scooby yelled. They jumped out of the car and saw Velma standing next to it.

"Like, don't do that!" Shaggy said.

"What's gotten into you two now?" Velma asked.

"Like, it's not what's gotten into us," Shaggy replied, "but what's gotten *after* us."

"Don't tell me you saw another wax monster chasing you?" Velma said.

"Not just any monster," Shaggy said. "It was him. Frankenstein's monster."

"Rike ris," Scooby barked.

Scooby stood up on his back legs and walked around stiffly like Frankenstein's monster. "Raaaaaaaarrrrrr," Scooby moaned.

"Hey, that's pretty good, Scoob," Shaggy said.

"Rank rou." Scooby smiled.

Velma peered into the other room.

"I don't see anyone in there now," she said. "But that's okay, because things are starting to fall into place."

"I'm getting that feeling, too," Fred said. He and Daphne walked through the doorway at the back of the exhibit. "Look what we found."

Fred held out a small black bag with a shoulder strap. Inside was an empty jewelry case.

"Where did you find it?" Velma asked.

"In the service corridor that connects all of the exhibits," Daphne replied.

"Just as I thought," Velma said. "Take a look at what we found next to the Frankenstein's monster wax dummy." She showed Fred and Daphne the green makeup stick.

"Are you thinking what I'm thinking, Fred?" Velma asked.

"I sure am, Velma," Fred replied. "And that means that it's time to set a trap."

"A trap to catch Frankenstein's monster?" Shaggy asked.

"Of course," Daphne replied.

"That's what I thought," Shaggy said. "Just don't forget one important thing."

"What shouldn't we forget?" Daphne said.

"To leave me and Scooby out!" Shaggy said.

Chapter 8

"According to what Madame Gaspacho said," Fred began, "no one can leave the building without her key."

"So we'll use the key as the bait," Velma continued. "Daphne and I will go get the key from Madame Gaspacho."

"And Shaggy, Scooby, and I will set up the rest of the trap," Fred said.

"Like, no way, man," Shaggy said. "Scooby and I have had enough frights in this castle of creepiness."

"But we need your help," Daphne said.

"Rorget it!" Scooby barked.

"Will you help us out for a Scooby Snack?" Daphne asked.

"Ruh-uh," Scooby said, shaking his head.

"How about two?" Velma asked

"Roo? Rokay!" he barked.

Velma reached into her pocket and then tossed two Scooby Snacks high into the air. Scooby jumped up and gobbled them down. Then Velma and Daphne left to get the key from Madame Gaspacho.

"Now here's the plan," Fred said. "We'll put the key around your neck, Scooby. You'll wait around the 'Movie Monsters' exhibit. When Frankenstein's monster shows up, lure him into this room. Shaggy and I will be hiding in the car. When the monster runs in, we'll throw this blanket over him."

Velma and Daphne returned with the key. They put it around Scooby's neck.

"Good luck, pal," Shaggy said.

Fred and Shaggy hid in the car. Velma and Daphne walked with Scooby back to the "Movie Monsters" exhibit in the next room.

"That was smart thinking on Madame Gaspacho's part to let Scooby hold the key," Daphne said loudly.

"You're right, Daphne," Velma agreed. "That way, she doesn't have to worry about Frankenstein's monster going after her and the countess."

"I just hope he doesn't find Scooby," Daphne added. Then Velma and Daphne hid behind some fake tombstones on the other side of the room.

A moment later, Scooby heard footsteps.

"Gulp!" Scooby swallowed hard.

Scooby turned and saw Frankenstein's monster walking toward him. The monster reached out to grab the key from around Scooby's neck. Scooby ducked out of the way. He ran over to the doorway to the "Inventors" exhibit in the next room.

Frankenstein's monster took a few steps toward Scooby.

"Go on, Scooby!" Daphne and Velma

called. "Go into the room."

"Right!" Scooby barked. He ran through the doorway.

But instead of following Scooby, the monster started walking toward the tombstones.

"Uh-oh," Daphne said. "I think he's after us now."

"Then it's time for Plan B," Velma said.

"What's Plan B?" asked Daphne.

"Run!" Velma exclaimed. Daphne and Velma stood up and ran into the "Inventors" exhibit.

Fred and Shaggy took their positions.

"Now!" Fred called. He and Shaggy stood up and threw the blanket into the air. It landed right on top of Velma and Daphne.

"Oh, no!" Fred exclaimed. "We've captured the girls!"

"That means Frankenstein's monster is still out there!" Shaggy said. "And here he comes!"

Fred, Shaggy, and Scooby saw the monster walk into the room.

"Aaaaaarrrrrrggggggghhhhh!" the monster moaned.

"Quick, Scooby, do something!" Shaggy called.

"Right!" Scooby barked.

Scooby ran over to Frankenstein's monster. The monster reached out to grab him. Scooby ducked and ran in circles around the monster. Then he ran between the monster's legs and back into the other room.

Frankenstein's monster lurched back into the "Movie Monsters" exhibit. He walked right by Scooby, who was posing as a wax figure. Scooby stood perfectly still as the monster looked around the room. But suddenly,

Scooby felt an itch on his nose.

"Rah-ah-ah-aaaaaaaa-chooooooby-Dooby-Doo!" sneezed Scooby.

The force of Scooby's sneeze knocked over the Wolfman statue. The Wolfman statue knocked over the Dracula statue. And the Dracula statue knocked over Frankenstein's monster.

"Arrrrrrrrggghh!" the monster yelled as he fell.

The rest of the gang ran into the room. They found the monster pinned under Dracula, with Scooby sitting on top.

"Good work, Scoob!" Shaggy said.

Chapter 9

Madame Gaspacho and the countess ran into the exhibit room.

"We heard a commotion," the countess said.

Madame Gaspacho looked around the exhibit.

"My statues!" she cried. "Look at my wax beauties lying on the floor!"

"All I care about is the necklace-stealing monster lying on the floor," the countess said.

"Countess, would you like to see who's

behind the mystery?" Fred asked.

"It would be my pleasure," the countess replied. She reached over and pulled off the monster's mask.

"Brant Embers!" the countess exclaimed. "You stole my necklace?"

"Just as we suspected," Fred said. "Though not at first."

"Fred's right," Velma added. "First we thought that Hank Harberg had something to do with it."

"Me?" Hank asked as he ran in. He was

trying to take his lens cap off but ended up unscrewing the whole lens. "Why me?"

"Because you made it clear that you wanted a good story for your paper," Daphne said. "We've seen some journalists do some pretty strange things for a story."

"But then we saw you help Madame Gaspacho take care of the countess," Velma continued. "A real thief wouldn't want to be so close to his victim."

"That left Mr. Tock and Brant Embers," Fred said. "They both sounded pretty unhappy with their bosses."

"This clue really confused us," Velma said. She held up a small black bag with a shoulder strap.

"Hey, that looks just like my camera bag!" Hank said.

"It also looks like the bag Mr.

Tock uses for his cell phone," the countess added.

"And the one Brant uses for his supplies when he needs to touch up a wax statue," Madame Gaspacho said.

"We found it in the service corridor connecting all of the exhibits," Velma said. "That meant that our fake Frankenstein's monster knew how to get around the museum quickly."

"Something Brant Embers would know from working here," Daphne said.

"And Mr. Tock would also know from checking out the museum's security for the countess's visit," Velma said.

"The thing that tipped us off was the empty jewelry box we found inside the black bag," Fred continued. "It was just the right size for the necklace."

"Information that both Mr. Tock and Brant Embers would know," the countess said.

"The only difference is that Mr. Tock

didn't know you were going to wear the real necklace today," Fred said.

"When we put this clue together with the green makeup stick we found," Velma said, "it all added up to Brant Embers."

"Why did you do this, Brant?" Madame Gaspacho asked. "After all I've done for you and your career."

"You've done nothing for my career but ruin it!" Brant snapped back. "When I came here I was a gifted artist and sculptor. I helped make you rich and famous. But you took all of the credit and honor for yourself. I had nothing. I stole the necklace so I could sell it. I was going to use the money to set up my own art studio on some remote tropical island. And I would have gotten away with it, too. Except those nosy kids and their meddling dog ruined everything."

Just then, Mr. Tock walked into the room.

"Countess, I'm sorry to say I've had no luck locating your necklace," he said sadly.

"That's all right, Tock," the countess said. "These fine young people cracked the case all by themselves."

"Really?" Mr. Tock said with surprise.

"That reminds me," the countess said. "If you would be so kind, Mr. Embers . . ."

She reached out her hand. Brant reached into his Frankenstein's monster costume and took out the necklace. He handed it to the countess.

"I'll go call the police," Madame Gaspacho said.

"How about it, Countess?" Hank asked. "How about a picture now?"

"Certainly," she replied. "But not just of me."

"No?" Hank asked.

"No, let's get our hero in the picture as well," the countess said. "Come, my friend."

Scooby jumped off Dracula and stood next to the countess. Just as Hank took the picture, Scooby gave the countess a great big Scooby kiss.

"Scooby!" Daphne scolded.

The countess laughed. "That's all right," she said. "He's not just any dog."

"He's my pal!" Shaggy cheered.

"Scooby-Dooby-Doo!" barked Scooby.

Solve a Mystery With Scooby-Doo!

SCOOBY-DOO! MYSTERIES

by James Gelsey

Ruh-roh!

Zoinks!